I Like Holidays!

WHAT IS THANKSGIVING?

Elaine Landau

Enslow Elementary
an imprint of
Enslow Publishers, Inc.
40 Industrial Road
Box 398
Berkeley Heights, NJ 07922
USA
http://www.enslow.com

CONTENTS

WORDS TO KNOW

feast—A very large meal that is greatly enjoyed.

holiday—A day of celebration.

Pilgrims—People from England who moved to Plymouth, Massachusetts, in 1620.

A SPECIAL TIME

A turkey is in the oven.
Vegetables are on the stove.
A pumpkin pie is ready.
What day is it? It must be
Thanksgiving!

THE START

It was the year 1620. Some people from England came to America. They wanted a new home. These people were Pilgrims. They started a new life in New England. But would they be able to live in this place during a cold winter?

RUDD. Sc.

SOME HELP

American Indians had lived in America for a long time. They gave the Pilgrims food. They taught them how to fish and hunt. In the spring, the Indians showed which plants would grow well. Then the Pilgrims could eat the food from the plants.

A GOOD HARVEST

The Pilgrims grew corn, squash, and beans. They learned which wild fruits and berries were safe to eat. The Pilgrims knew they would have enough food for the winter. They planned a feast.

THANKSGIVING FEAST

The feast lasted three days. Pilgrims and American Indians came. They ate turkey, rabbit, and deer. They also ate corn, pumpkin, and berries. People may have eaten eel, codfish, and clams. They played games. They had races, too.

THANKSGIVING GOES ON

Today we still enjoy this holiday. It comes on the fourth Thursday in November. Family and friends visit. They come from near and far. They eat lots of good food.

MORE
TO DO

Some people go to parades. Others go to football games. Families bring food to people who do not have enough to eat. It is a day to share. It is a day to celebrate.

MACY'S
THANKSGIVING DAY
PARADE
MACY'S
THANKSGIVING DAY
PARADE

THANKSGIVING MEANS A LOT

It is a time to think about all that we have. We are lucky to have a place to live and food to eat. We are thankful for our friends and family. It is a great holiday!

WHAT YOU CAN DO: AN ACTIVITY

Our families love and care for us all year. Other people help us stay safe, too. Police officers, firefighters, and school crossing guards help us. So do doctors and nurses.

Make a thank-you poster for someone you do not usually thank.

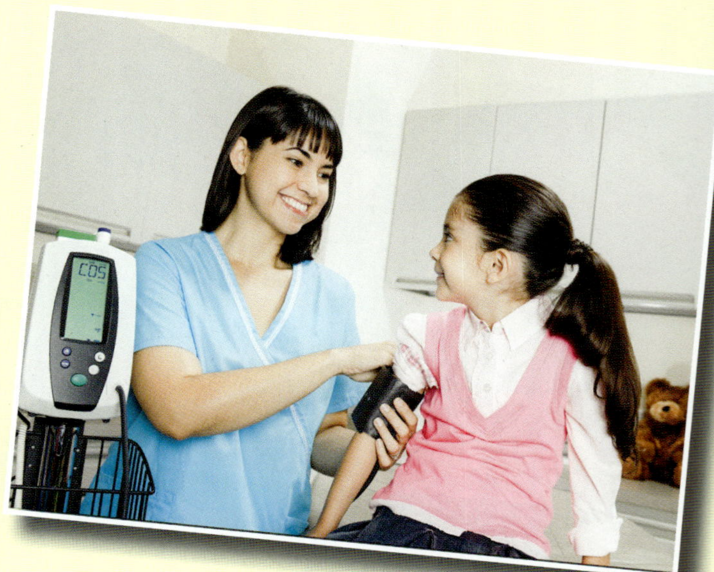

Decorate a piece of poster board. Add pictures that remind you of Thanksgiving. You can draw them or cut them from magazines. In the center of your poster write:

This Thanksgiving I'm thankful for you!

You (write in what that person does, for example: help keep us safe).

Thank you for doing this!

You can make the thank-you poster alone or with friends. Everyone who worked on it should sign his or her name. Give the poster to the person just before Thanksgiving. **EXPECT TO SEE A SMILE!**

LEARN MORE

BOOKS

Mercer, Abbie. *Happy Thanksgiving*. New York: PowerKids Press, 2007.

Peppas, Lynn. *Thanksgiving*. New York: Crabtree Publishers, 2009.

Ross, Kathy. *All New Crafts for Thanksgiving*. Minneapolis, Minn.: Millbrook Press, Inc., 2006.

Webster, Christine. *How to Draw Thanksgiving Symbols*. New York: PowerKids Press, 2005.

WEB SITES

The First Thanksgiving
<http://www.scholastic.com/scholastic_thanksgiving>

Thanksgiving Activies
<http://holidays.kaboose.com/thanksgiving/>

INDEX

Enslow Elementary, an imprint of Enslow Publishers, Inc.

Enslow Elementary® is a registered trademark of Enslow Publishers, Inc.

Library of Congress Cataloging-in-Publication Data

Landau, Elaine.

What is Thanksgiving? / Elaine Landau.

p. cm. — (I like holidays!)

Includes index.

ISBN 978-0-7660-3701-4

1. Thanksgiving Day—Juvenile literature. I. Title.

GT4975.L36 2012

394.2649—dc22

2010020883

Paperback ISBN 978-1-59845-294-5

Printed in the United States of America

032012 Lake Book Manufacturing, Inc., Melrose Park, IL

10 9 8 7 6 5 4 3 2

To Our Readers: We have done our best to make sure all Internet Addresses in this book were active and appropriate when we went to press. However, the author and the publisher have no control over and assume no liability for the material available on those Internet sites or on other Web sites they may link to. Any comments or suggestions can be sent by e-mail to comments@enslow.com or to the address on the back cover.

Enslow Publishers, Inc., is committed to printing our books on recycled paper. The paper in every book contains 10% to 30% post-consumer waste (PCW). The cover board on the outside of each book contains 100% PCW. Our goal is to do our part to help young people and the environment too!

Photo Credits: Associated Press, p. 17; Enslow Publishers, Inc., p. 6; © Frances Roberts/Alamy, p. 16; Monkey Business Images /Shutterstock.com, pp. 3 (middle), 14; iStockphoto.com: Bhofack2/iStock/Thinkstock, pp. 3(top), 19; Image Source/ DigitalVision/Getty Images, p. 1; © Sean Locke, p. 20; Library of Congress, pp. 3 (bottom), 7, 13; Nativestock Pictures/Photolibrary, p. 11; © North Wind/North Wind Picture Archives, p. 8; Stockbyte/Getty Images, p. 4; Shutterstock.com, pp. 2, 5, 18, 21, 23; Steve Hix/Fuse/Corbis/Getty Images, p. 20

Cover Photo: Shutterstock.com

Series Consultant:
Duncan R. Jamieson, PhD
Professor of History
Ashland University
Ashland, OH

Series Literacy Consultant:
Allan A. De Fina, PhD
Dean, College of Education/Professor of Literacy Education
New Jersey City University
Past President of the New Jersey Reading Association